The Christmas Before Brexit

E R Forsberg

Text copyright © 2018

All Rights Reserved

ISBN-13: 978-1545216484

ISBN-10: 1545216487

Published by *Red Revenant*

To welfare reformers everywhere:

Mutato nomine de te fabula narrator.

Horace, Satires, I. 1. 69.

The worst sin towards our fellow creatures is not to hate them, but to be indifferent to them: that's the essence of inhumanity.

GB Shaw, The Devil's Disciple

Prologue

For a devout minority, Christ-tide – as the Puritans called it - remained a time to venerate the birth of a saviour and share a message of peace and love to all. For the many, alas, the sacred name and origin had been lost in a circus of commercial and hedonistic rites. Enjoyment of the season had become a private preserve to be experienced and enjoyed in the name of individuality; either as conspicuous consumption or in church services that offered personal salvation wrapped in a naïf pastoral scene.

And so, it was, in the Age of Austerity. The festive focus on families and socialising, the reunion of relatives and friends near and far in a spirit of companionship and mutual goodwill, had given way to a self-gratifying orgy of the super-rich. Possessions replaced blessings, offering only short lived satisfaction, to be sought over and over again in the name of fashion. No endearing mementoes of childhood or heavenly happiness here to reflect beams of innocent joy, or a glimmer of divine beneficence.

Still, there were some who endeavoured to provide a fleeting happiness to those least able to withstand the icy blast of state sponsored privation. In dim lit halls, undernourished persons were offered sanctuary from the wrenching spirit with which men, indifferent to the season's intrinsic nature, looked only for gain. Eyes that had long since ceased to shine with hope dared to glisten at the thought of peace and good-will replacing avarice and hard dealing.

Here at least, charitable dispositions stirred acts of compassion for those whose hearts were heavy with worldly cares and sorrows. Generous and kind, they reached out with a merry voice and smiling face to extend the warmth of the festive season, in keeping with the Golden Rule:

Do unto others, as you would be done by.

I

Known as the quiet man who had tried so hard to get louder, he remained as mean and mealy mouthed as any politician could be. Hopes of attaining the great offices of state had been dashed on the barren rocks of a one-dimensional personality. Dreams of greatness had come to nought and he could have no doubt that it had been an ignominious fall. The newspapers, television, radio and social media were there to remind him, lest he should try to forget.

He was the chief, the only mourner at that particular passing. Not many ordinary folk noticed and still fewer cared, but on that very day he resolved that they would be made to pay for his disappointment. He didn't know how many years it would take, but one day to be sure he would make others feel the pain, anguish and desolation that he had felt at his miserable demise. He had no doubt about this. For at the precise moment that his hopes of glory died, the milk of human kindness evaporated from his every pore. It might be said that from that day he was left without feeling but that would be untrue. He still had one feeling: an overwhelming desire for revenge.

It was said that the foolhardy could be taken in by his kindly countenance. His rounded face, reassuring smile and sleek head concealed a heart of stone. Some had gone so far as to say that he had more than a passing resemblance to the avuncular Alistair Sim, but the ice like stare of his cold blue eyes betrayed the iron within, while the reed-like voice sang of the shrivelled hopes that twisted and tormented him daily. As time went on, his obsession with wealth and status made him surly, morose and lonely, giving him more of a forlorn expression.

Each friendly face was greeted with a scowl of distrust, while the impertinent poor were treated with disdain, simply because they had the cheek to breathe the same air as he. It was no wonder then, that he preferred his own company, had to even, as he left every acquaintance feeling that they had been buffeted by the foulest of winter weather. Even the casual passer-by felt despoiled by the shroud of bitterness in which he wrapped himself; in much the same way as a leaf is left burnt by an encounter with frost or snow.

Perhaps it was because or in spite of his proclivities that his fortunes changed when at long last a place in Government became his. Indeed, Secretary of State for Wrack and Ruin, was the ideal position for him to put his punitive plans into practice. If a person fell on hard times, their misfortune would be his opportunity. He would grasp it with both hands, turn their noses to the grind-stone and squeeze the living daylight out of any poor defenceless wretch that fell upon his mercy. It mattered not to him if they were able bodied, sick or old. Poor, they were and poor they would remain, so long as they had the cheek to live at another's expense.

In weaker moments, he thought he experienced a fleeting feeling of pleasure at his new-found role, but it had been so long since he felt that emotion that he could not be sure what the sensation was. Just to be on the safe side, he decided to repress it, lest it betray his plans, change his nature or forestall this, his last great hope. If he had been born in an earlier time, he mused, when the Poor Law had been in full flow, his manners and customs would not have been regarded as peculiar.

But in the end, he didn't care. In fact, he liked nothing better than to walk amongst the destitute to test the strength of his resilience to human suffering and misery. He even found that it helped to kindle his zeal for the battle against the host of hellish foes, real or imaginary, with whom he planned to do combat. It made sure that no degree of human suffering was sufficient to crack his deep-rooted resolve to exact a bitter revenge on all who burdened the public purse.

He took great pride in following the courtier's custom of kicking whoever their royal masters kicked whenever he encountered the mendicant poor. They were subjected to the wrath of his tongue, before the long arm of the law was called upon to punish them further. If he had any say in the matter, he would have them say of him: 'There goes Smith. He hates us everyone.'

Now, it had occurred to him that there was no better time of year to experience the misery of want than on good old Christmas-eve. And, that there was no better place for such an adventure than at a food bank or a church hall where a festive dinner was being served free of charge. Of course, he would make it known to the organisers, lest there be any doubt, that he was not there to help provide a much-needed dole. Neither was he there to extol the credo of companionship and goodwill, nor to offer respite, however brief, from the restless struggles of existence, from the worries and distresses of the world.

Oh, no! His purpose was to turn a churlish cheek to fellow beings as they met and mimicked what they imagined to be the celebration of Christmas amongst the better off.

II

Now it might be thought that old Smith had mellowed with age, simply because he had allowed another to indulge herself in his festive pastime. This was no casual observer mind you. It was none other than McVain, Minister of State for Exploitation. Some said her strangulated features had been wrought from icicles forged inside her uncaring body, but no one knew where the long golden locks came from.

Like him, she was not one to derive pleasure from the beauty of nature. She had never looked up to the sky to feel the warmth of the sun on her face, or to wonder at the depths of the fathomless nitrous ocean above, upon which fleets of clouds sailed. Never had she enjoyed the aural luxury of hearing birds sing. Neither had she tasted the subtle freshness of spring, the voluptuous green of summer or the earthiness of autumn.

If for some reason, she had to walk along a crowded path, she did so frigidly and with head bowed, looking up only to grimace a warning, more awful than words could express, for others to keep their distance. Such were the qualities she shared with Smith, along with a predilection for the most expensive clothes and a deep distrust of the hoi polloi.

And so it was that on 24th December, they left Caxton House, Tothill Street, London in their chauffer driven limousine and headed off to an obscure part of town. Partly to protect their anonymity and partly to add a sense of danger, they decided to go somewhere they had never visited before, an area with a bad reputation. As their destination grew near, they marvelled at the litter strewn narrow streets, sneered at the run-down houses and charity shops and pointed at the waifs, sullen, unhealthy and mean in appearance.

Eventually the car pulled up at an old warehouse, now used by the Trussel Trust and, getting out, the Ministers were greeted by a mild-mannered volunteer with an honest face and a broad smile that beamed a kindly welcome. Neither reciprocated, as they brushed contemptuously past the girl and entered a large room. Blast after icy blast of wintry wind rushed through gaps in the doors and window casements. All the better, thought Smith, this should not be a place of comfort and joy; unless of course one had the benefit of an Armani coat in cashmere blend.

Outside, unseen phantom figures could be heard beating their hands and stamping their feet in an attempt to generate some warmth. They had queued for over an hour now, having been made to wait for their tormentors to arrive. Some were hopeful, others grateful, but few contented. Many of those waiting had eyes that told a tale of woe as they peered through dirty windows into a room filled with the faint glow and false warmth of electric light.

At last, the door of the Food Bank was opened and the waiting souls trudged in, wearing clothes that were thread-bare, scanty and patched, and shoes unfit for winter weather; much to the amusement of the watching harpies who nudged each other and sniggering, pointed out the most desperate figures. Standing warm in luxuriant apparel, their breath turned to mist as it touched the cold air of the room. No such effect was visible from those in the passing line. They had barely enough body heat to sustain them.

"A merry Christmas and God bless you both" one of the most downtrodden mumbled in a low voice. McVain cackled and clutched at Smith's arm. "What's that?" barked Smith "A claimant on barely fifteen shillings a week wishing us a merry Christmas? Someone take their name! I'll have their benefit stopped." McVain cackled again "Oh yes, please do!" she squealed in delight through her drooping mouth.

One of the assistants handing out food parcels overheard their exchange: "Stop their benefit? Surely you don't mean that Mr Smith?"

"I do," said Smith "They have no right to be merry when they are living off the charity of others. If they have reason to be merry, then they are not poor enough."

"Are you saying that only the rich have a right to be merry at Christmas sir?"

"Oh yes, yes, yes!" McVain chimed in excitedly "the richer the better."

"Then why are you both so miserable, uncharitable and unchristian, is it that you are not rich enough?"

"Not rich enough, not rich enough" McVain sang in her shrill voice as she swayed on Smith's arm.

"What else can we be, when we live in a world full of fools?" asked Smith as he tried to detach himself from the now hysterical McVain "If a person expects to live without paying bills, they should know what it is like to live without money. I don't see why they should be allowed to keep Christmas in their own way. So long as they are on benefit and living at the taxpayer's expense they should keep it in mine."

"Keep it! Keep it!" chattered McVain mindlessly.

"Of course, they don't have to keep it all. Maybe they would be better to leave it alone, for all the good it has ever done them."

"Leave it! Leave it!" The delirium continued at his side, until it had become too much for Smith and he shouted "McVain!" to bring his accomplice to heel.

The Food Bank supervisor now joined the conversation. "Are you saying that the only good that can be derived from something, is in the form of a profit? Is not Christmas, with its sacred story and message a good time for all? Are all those who try to be kind, forgiving, charitable and pleasant at this time of year, really just fools?"

"In my eyes, they are."

"It is for just one day of the year. Can it be so wrong to ponder the plight of the less fortunate?"

"Of course not, that is why we are here" quipped Smith scornfully.

"To see them suffer and to revel in their human tragedy, you mean?"

Knowing full well that they had entered through a side entrance, the supervisor continued: "Did you not see the inscription at the entrance? It is Matthew 25:42-43:

'For I was a hungry, and ye gave me no meat: I was thirsty, and ye gave me no drink:

I was a stranger, and ye took me not in: naked, and ye clothed me not: sick, and in prison, and ye visited me not.'

We are all destined for the grave, rich and poor, great and low. What reason will you give for this behaviour on the day of judgement?"

"Fairy tale nonsense and nothing more is my answer. It is all humbug I tell you!" snarled Smith.

"Humbug! Humbug!" the demented cheerleader resumed her cacophony.

"A speaker with your gift for hot air and bluster would not be out of place in Parliament."

"But I fear that my conscience would be. You are more likely to see me in the line with these poor people before you see me in that house of the self-righteous and self-seeking."

"The choice is yours. Everyone here has chosen their own destiny of their own free will."

"Does that include you too sir? Were you denied great office by others or did you deny yourself?"

"How dare you!" growled Smith. "Come McVain, we will be better entertained at one of our job centres. The people there will know their place."

"Can I have one as a pet?" McVain begged Smith as they left "I promise I'd be horrid to it."

Without further ado, he shoved her into the back of the waiting limousine. The driver closed the door behind them and awaited instructions.

III

With the journey to the job centre underway, Smith relaxed into the plush leather seats and adopted his favourite vacant expression. McVain fidgeted with her hair, pouted vacuously and gazed at her reflection in the window next to her - as much reflection as misanthropic ice casts on glass, that is.

All was quiet until Smith suddenly came to life and shouted "Stop the car!"

Thinking there had been an accident, the driver slammed on the brakes and McVain was catapulted onto the floor with a shriek. As quick as a flash Smith opened the door and leapt into action. Unbeknown to the others, his quarry was a homeless person with a dog, whom he had spotted sitting in a shop doorway. He ran over to them and kicked away a paper cup containing loose change, scattering its contents across the pavement.

"What right have you to litter these streets and inconvenience decent shoppers going about their lawful business? I want nothing from you, so why do you demand something of me? Be gone and take that mangy mutt with you."

Not the most agile of people, Smith fashioned a lumbering kick at the dog, but before he could execute his wicked deed, the hound bared its teeth and snarled as if in the presence of pure evil. Now, it is often said that animals are a better judge of character than people and it might be true in Smith's case, because be they mongrel, puppy or pedigree all dogs conjured up the same response to his presence. Even timid cats were given to hissing and spitting at him.

The poor man, on the other hand, looked terrified. His eyes were wide with fear as he collected together the blanket that had kept him and his dog warm and scrambled after the scattered change. Until, that is, Smith turned on him again, pushed him back into the doorway and rapped him over the head with his glove; as if challenging him to a duel.

To the Minister of Wrack and Ruin, his intervention was the source of whole-hearted self-satisfaction and, in a state of contented splendour, he made his way back to the waiting limousine. Even the laughs and cheerful shouts of those making bustling preparations for the next day's cheer were not enough to dent the gall and wormwood in his heart.

His face even appeared to beam in the golden light that glowed through the shop windows and, for the first time in some while, it was almost as if he had a spring in his step. He was brushing imaginary dust from his coat and reliving his triumph to himself, when McVain brought him back to the present. Now back on the seat, she leaned out of the door chirruping: "Did you punch him? Did you kick him?"

There was no reply. He merely pushed her back into the car with almost as much contempt as had been shown to the destitute specimens of creation. Then in a quiet, self-satisfied, yet nasal voice he ordered his chauffeur: "Drive on."

When they arrived at the Job Centre, they again entered by means of a rear door. The office manager was there to greet them with an obsequious bow, so low his nose seemed to touch the floor. Still genuflecting, he walked backwards into the public area and was followed by the processing Smith and McVain, who were once again basking in their own self-importance.

Without warning, the sound of a choir began to fill the air:

"God bless you, merry gentleman!

May nothing you dismay!"

The first few lines had barely been uttered before Smith became indignant at the hearing of a jolly song and shouted: "What is the meaning of this?"

"It is a local choir, sir. They like to give a festive touch to the day, it being Christmas eve."

"Get them away from here" ordered Smith "What could be more ridiculous than wishing a merry Christmas to the deserving poor?"

"Wishing a merry Christmas to the undeserving poor" McVain chimed in, before she caught sight of Smith's disdainful stare.

"Are you against any such liberality sir" the manager enquired giving the gibbering McVain a wide berth.

"Liberality is, as liberality does" said Smith, frowning and shaking his head in disapproval

"Everything has its time and place. Liberality is good for the economy and an incentive to work harder, which is what these wastrels should be looking to do."

"Would you expect them to continue looking during this most festive of seasons, even when many businesses are closed?" asked a would-be carol singer standing at the door. "Do not the poor and destitute need support at a time of privation?" he continued. "And does not the same apply to those who are in work and still in want of basic necessities, not to mention comfort."

"Then they should work harder."

"And if they can't?"

"Then there are food banks, charitable organisations and hostels they can rely on."

"They are very busy, sir. Some might say too busy to offer sufficient to eat and drink, let alone a Christian message."

"Then their utility remains unimpaired. The country cannot afford to make idle people merry. They cost enough as it is. If they are in as bad a state as you and they claim, they will be grateful for whatever they get."

"And if they cannot get enough, would you decide which ones shall live and which might die?"

"Die!" screeched Smith raising his voice "There is no reason for them to die, but if they are intent on it they will at least help us to reduce the claimant count. That is my business and nothing more. I see no reason to interfere with the course of people's lives."

"It seems to me that not interfering is your business" the carol singer chided "so that want can be experienced by the many and abundance by the few. Whither the business of charity, mercy, forbearance and benevolence? For who in the sight of Heaven is more worthless and less fit to live – you or the poor?"

At this point, the office manager intervened and closed the door on the carol singer and Smith turned to McVain with an expression that conveyed a mixture of arrogance and contempt: "They should forbear their wicked cant until they understand how the surplus is created and for whose benefit it should therefore be employed" he opined.

Still trying to rescue the situation, the manager invited them into the back office, but his hopes were dashed by the appearance of two minions distributing sherry and mince pies. Catching sight of Smith and McVain they approached and held out their trays. Smith dismissed the pies with a disdainful flick of his right hand, but surprisingly took a glass of sherry. He cut an effete figure, holding his glass in a gloved hand and raising it to barely touch his pouting lips.

McVain on the other hand, showed no such reserve. She took both trays and placed them on top of a nearby cabinet, before starting to chomp her way through the mince pies. Crumbs flew from her gnashing jaws as she seemed unable to eat and breathe at the same time. She did, however, manage to consume the sherry without spilling it, perhaps to help down any undigested pastry.

Either way, it wasn't long before she was leaning heavily against the cabinet, her dark crumpled coat a firmament of sugar crystals and crumbs. Her previously sharp features were now so relaxed that they took on the appearance of melting wax and her mouth sagged heavily at each corner. Then without warning she slid slowly down the front of the cabinet and came to rest in a pitiful heap on the floor.

Smith had seen enough. Repulsed by its inferior quality, he placed his almost untouched sherry on the nearest available surface and turned to leave. The manager tried to revive McVain, but it was to no avail. It took three people to raise her back onto her feet, but by that time Smith had gone, leaving her to her own devices.

IV

Bristling with fury Smith flounced onto the back seat of the waiting car and ordered the driver to take him home. Next, he took out his phone and rang his housekeeper: 'I'll be home in 45 and expect a hot punch and delicacies upon arrival' he sneered in to the device. With his instructions given, he slumped back in the seat and allowed his overcoat to slip open as he gazed inanely at the strife and tumult of city life going on outside.

By now it was late afternoon and the temperature was falling fast, causing a film of mist to collect on the car windows. It gave the impression of an external fog, made orange by sodium street lights and turned the cars, buses and lorries into shadows as they jostled for the way in the busy thoroughfares of London. In the near distance the Christmas dressings of the shop windows beckoned the unwary to waste their lives in getting and spending, not that a Tory Minister bothered himself with such trifles.

Smith watched the would-be bargain hunters through the hazy glass and amused himself with the thought that they were little more than ghostly apparitions of the poor wandering and wondering at the delights they could not afford. He chuckled inwardly at their restless state and imagined them moaning and groaning at their disappointment.

All of a sudden, what had been a pleasant interlude was interrupted by a face pressed against the window. Expressionless and haunting, it reminded Smith of that painting by Edvard Munch and he assumed it was a mendicant migrant about to assail him for money. Filled with contempt he was about to order the driver to put his foot down and run over the wraith, when he realised that it was McVain.

She had been able to catch them as they waited in rush hour traffic and the biting cold had sobered her senses. It was Smith's instinct to abandon her to the fickle fortunes of fate but, before he could speak, the driver had realised who it was and had opened a door. Humbled by her experience she slipped into the car without a word, although she did seem to wear an embarrassed smile.

Looking straight ahead Smith began to drone to no-one in particular: "No doubt the people we observed today considered themselves ill used, but our work is for their own good. What we are about is fairness for all and making work pay. Not that you would know it from the reaction we get from these ungrateful ne'er-do-wells. They accuse us of pride, ill-will, hatred, envy, bigotry and selfishness, but these things are theirs and not ours.

"As regrettable as it may be, we do not have the power of life and death. It is the process of natural selection that decides who will or will not live and if the judgement happens to fall upon the poor the most, it is because they deserve it most. Perhaps they would be happier, more content with their lot, if they knew the truth of it.

"They held us responsible for the dangers faced by miners as they toiled in the bowels of the earth and for the fishermen who braved the thundering tempest and the dangers of the deep to earn their living. It was our liberal economics that saved them from their perils, but did they thank us for it? No, they blamed us for the fact that they needed to look for work."

No-one paid any attention to his ramblings. The driver had used headphones to reduce the effects of the tinnitus-like voice. McVain meanwhile had succumbed to the heated deep pile seats, and reverted to her semi-conscious state, drooling from both sides of her mouth.

Time passed slowly as Smith continued to think out loud. Until, that is, the car approached the multi-million-pound Tudor mansion where our servant of the people enjoyed a vigorous prosperity at the expense of his wife's family and the taxpayer. Not that he cared about that. Much more important to him was the fact that the ancestral pile encompassed a stream, tennis courts, orchards, swimming pools and a deer park.

In summer, a muster of peacocks strutted on the manicured lawn and perched splendidly on the antique stone balustrades, urns and statues, betwixt and between flower-beds, clipped shrubberies and raised terraces. The birds were

Smith's particular favourites, introduced by him, to provide a sense of finery, pomp and magnificence in keeping with his aristocratic pretensions.

The Estate was protected against the intrusion of riff-raff by a pair of magnificent iron gates, fancifully wrought with flourishes and flowers and supported by huge square columns surmounted with the family crest. After passing the second line of defence, a porter's lodge buried out of sight in dense shrubbery, the car wound its way through a noble avenue of trees toward a lawn sheeted in frost and veiled in a thin shroud of opaque vapour.

There in the distance stood the house. Courtly and venerable, the smoke from its chimneys formed dark organic columns that rose in strong relief against the clear, cold sky. Closer to earth, a dark shadow of yew trees protected a mansion that, illuminated by pale moonlight, was wont to reveal itself through diamond-shaped panes of glass that glistered in stone-shafted, crenelated bay windows.

As the car drew up before the main entrance, the driver removed his ear pieces and awaited instruction. "I suppose you'd better take the whole day off tomorrow" said Smith, "don't worry about me I will make whatever arrangements are necessary. Just take McVain to her latest domicile on your way home."

There was no reply, or if there was it was drowned out by the crunching of gravel as the car turned, and sped along the drive. Smith didn't care. It was least said, soonest mended with servants as far as he was concerned.

Relieved to be returning to a standard of life he considered to be his God given right, Smith passed swiftly through the large oak door; hung on strap hinges and dotted with the heads of handmade nails. He then entered a spacious foyer, which was warmed by a blazing fire to the right and adorned with an ornate staircase that boasted inlaid treads and landings. On a side table, he noticed that his new ministerial diary had arrived and, taking it with him as he went in search of his punch and delicacies, he flicked through the pages, pondering the next instalment of his war on the great unwashed.

V

Undecorated walls, cold and frugal, in passages used by the members of staff, gave no indication of the season. Some concessions were visible in the wainscoted hall, where the oaken gallery, mounted weaponry and hunting trophies from olden times were barely brightened with strands of evergreen. No such reticence was necessary in the less public quarters, however.

The larder overflowed with an abundance of flora and fauna: game, poultry, joints of meat, chains of sausages and shellfish for the carnivore. Sugar coated nuts, candied fruit, rich puddings and cakes for the sweet toothed. The olfactory senses danced to the tune of myriad savoury odours, that emanated from spices, coffee and exotic ingredients. Everything looked good to eat, but in pride of place was a magnificent pie. Decorated at one end with peacocks' feathers, in imitation of the tail, at the other lay the head, its beak dressed in gold leaf.

This theme of extravagance found fruition in a capacious study, where the floor was carpeted in a deep woollen pile and the walls bedecked with richly coloured tapestries. Intervening bookshelves were loaded with portfolio editions of leather-bound dusty tomes, the pages of which had not seen the light of day in a long time. It was in such pretentious surroundings that Smith was often to be found, ensconced in a large hereditary elbow-chair, pondering the paragraphs and clauses of social security legislation, endeavouring to concoct new schemes of cruelty.

Here the season was well marked. Sprigs of holly and other evergreens adorned portraits, candelabra and other fixtures, festooned with bright red berries. Crisp green leaves reflected light from Christmas candles wrapped in ivy and from the yule log that crackled and blazed in the prominent and wide-mouthed fireplace. Moreover, this conflict of flickering flames caused a huge silver vessel and its parade of goblets to sparkle like a galaxy of stars.

The vessel was a bowl of steaming punch that had been prepared in accordance with Smith's instructions and placed on a highly-polished table. It was concocted from the richest wines, was spiced with nutmeg, cinnamon and ginger, and sweetened by honey and roasted apples. All of which combined to give off a delicious aroma, just the thing to dispel any lingering thoughts of cold winter weather.

With a look of smug satisfaction, he stirred the mighty vessel and ladled its contents into a goblet. Leaning against the fireplace in a half-studied attitude he gazed at the enormous log that blazed in the hearth and sent forth a torrent of heat and light. This fallen tree was allowed to burn all night until, in keeping with ancient custom, the remaining brand was carefully put away to light the next year's Christmas fire.

But even such a scene was not enough to distract him from his pet project. His mood became a mixture of disapproval and vengeance, as he mused about a country overrun with vagrants. Collecting an old volume of legislation, so well read it could have been the index of his mind, he reclined in his mulberry coloured leather chair. Then, as was his custom, he opened it at random to take for a prophecy the first lines that met his eyes. In this way, he hoped to find something whereby he could add at least one more wrinkle to a brow of care, or beguile a destitute heart with further sorrow.

And on this particular day, in the early hours of Christmas morning, he was not disappointed by what he read:

'The personal representatives of a person who was in receipt of a benefit at any time before his death shall provide the Secretary of State with such information as he may require relating to the assets and liabilities of that person's estate.'

Immediately, he recognised the opportunity this offered for him to extend his web of torment. He felt like laughing and crying at the same time and to see him in such a heightened and excited state would have been a surprise to all who knew him in the governmental corridors of the City of London.

True enough, he was not able to pursue a claimant beyond the grave. They had escaped their worldly cares, but those who survived could be punished for the sins of the parent. Even before tears of grief had dried, while the bereaved were still sad, mournful and despairing he could strike. And there was no better place to do this from, than an incongruous location; somewhere like Mitcheldean in the wiles of Gloucestershire.

Now, it is well known that he was not much in the habit of cracking jokes, but he could not help recalling something that was said earlier in the day about being destined for the grave. In the light of his new project, there seemed to be something prophetic about it, and he allowed himself to become almost waggish. What if he was able to reduce bereavement allowance and grants for funeral costs, as well? Coffins would be more expensive and at Christmas time that would be his version of a Christmas box.

Feeling light-headed from the effects of punch and his unaccustomed frivolity, he reclined, closed his eyes and began to dream of the havoc he could create for people. First, he would have the Probate Registry notify his office as soon as a person who was in receipt of a means tested benefit had passed away. Then he would demand evidence of the deceased's income and savings from the start of their claim. Yes, and if the relatives couldn't provide the information he would claim the money back anyway. After all, benefits were not there to make people comfortable and he would make sure there could be no doubt about that.

VI

Before long, the effects of the roaring fire and brandy-laced elixir began to take their toll. Overcome by an irresistible drowsiness, Smith's last conscious thoughts were of an overwhelming heaviness that afflicted his limbs, his eye lids and then his brain. In other words, he sank into a deep sleep and began to dream.

Floating in a state of ecstasy, his mood was one of euphoric pleasure, of having neither care nor sorrow as he listened to strains of music that broke forth from an adjacent room. Until, without warning, the door swung open with such a bang that it felt as though the house had been struck by a thunderbolt. Then, the study was filled with a flash of light which, as it faded, revealed a surreal scene.

Peering through startled eyes, Smith was able to make out the interior of the Cabinet Room in Downing Street. He was in no doubt about that, but the table around which Government Ministers sat was loaded with a substantial display of seasonal abundance. Almost as impressive as his own larder, he thought.

But as soon as he had come to terms with this vision, he noticed that the music began to recede, to become softer and ethereal as if to herald some great event. The sense of anticipation only heightened as the music gave way to singing and then, suddenly, through an opposite door, Prime Minister Davy entered, all dressed up in his Bullingdon best, his shiny red face beaming radiantly like the sun. He was attended on either side by junior ministers, each bearing a large Yule Candle and, at waist height, he carried a silver salver with an enormous pig's head, its mouth facing toward him.

Behind followed a pageant of ministers dressed as characters from a Christmas masque. There was Pickles looking even more ridiculous than normal in tights, cloak and ruff, carrying a large basket of pies, to which he was helping himself. Hunt followed stooped and simpering in a long coat and drooping cap, that hung loosely from his gangly frame. Then came Johnson in a schoolboy's cap and uniform, looking for all the world like one of the Tweedle twins.

May was next in line, her waxy grey pallor exaggerated by dour domestic dress and not dissimilar to that of the large fish she carried in a dish. Both also wore the same open-mouthed expression, as if straining against hook and line. Finally, the star of the show was Osborne, dressed in a sparkling harlequin costume and grinning inanely, he came tumbling in a large hoop while juggling with bags of money.

To the casual observer such eccentricities, could be somewhat perplexing, but not Smith. He was a graduate of Sandhurst and used to many a peculiar ceremony. Furthermore, he had become acquainted with this particular custom during reminiscences by the Prime Minister and his Oxonian alumni. He recognised it as the ritual of the 'Communion with the Boar's Head.'

In fact, he was sick to death of hearing about the noble old Oxbridge college halls where students loitered in black gowns and, with an air of comic gravity, chanted the old carol now sung by the pageant of fools processing in his midst:

"The boar's head in hand bear I,
Bedeck'd with bays and rosemary;
And I pray you, my masters, be merry,
Quot estia in convivio.
Caput apri defero
Reddens laudes Domino.

The boar's head, as I understand,
Is the rarest dish in all this land,
Which thus bedeck'd with a gay garland
Let us servire cantico.
Caput apri defero,
Reddens laudes Domino.

Our Steward hath provided this
In honour of the King of Bliss,
Which here today we all shall know
Caput apri fallatio

Worst of all, the spectacle and the stories associated with it caused Smith great discomfort, as they served to remind him that, in reality, he was nothing but a hanger-on.

Perhaps that's why, as the Boar's head was placed with great formality at the head of the table, he found himself returned to consciousness by a loud snorting noise, not unlike sleep apnoea, but one that was nevertheless directed at the infernal scene. Whatever the reason, it made him sit up and attempt to collect his thoughts. Half-awake he tried to make sense of his confused recollections. He felt cold and nauseous, as people do when they have been roused unexpectedly from a drunken slumber and, getting to his feet gingerly, felt his way around the room as if to reassure himself of its identity.

With his wits restored, or as near as they could be at that point, he was overcome with a dread that something equally horrific was waiting for him beyond the confines of his study. He therefore prized the door ajar and peered out into the darkness, fearful that he should encounter another macabre vision.

Satisfied that the coast was clear, he relaxed a little and on tip toe crossed the hall and scuttled up the stairs to the hoped for safety of his bed.

VII

Although it was a journey he had made many times before, Smith flinched and shivered at every unfamiliar shadow. Even the old suits of armour, family portraits and ancestral busts took on a new and threatening demeanour in the pale moonlight of the early hours. Afraid to look ahead, he kept his head bowed until, gratefully, he reached the sheltered sanctuary of his chamber.

"Darkness might be cheap," he muttered to himself, "but it is better suited to the poor."

Now, to be fair to Smith, it has to be said that his place of slumber was more than a bedroom. It would more accurate to describe it as a grand and ornate suite set at the centre of his private wing. The entrance lobby was modest enough, but the withdrawing room could only be described as opulent.

With its original stone fireplace, the room was panelled with intricately carved cornices and featured a burr walnut centre table. This sumptuous theme continued into a separate room, where a lofty tester stood opposite floor to ceiling bay windows. Dressed in a rich red damask, the bed was complemented by a matching velvet chaise longue at its foot and in an adjoining bathroom Carrara marble had been used to create the desired level of luxury.

Even amidst the security of such familiar surroundings, Smith was not in an agreeable state. He shivered and wiped the perspiration from his brow as he inspected each room to make sure that everything was as it should be. He looked under the table, under the couch and under the bed, before approaching his dressing-gown with caution as it hung menacingly on the back of a door.

Next, he returned to the entrance and locked the door to secure himself against surprise. Then he locked his bedroom door, though this was not his custom, in an attempt to feel doubly secure. Thus satisfied, he put on his favourite Swiss pyjamas, hand stitched in a woven cotton and satin voile, feather-light on the skin, finished with golden piping and mother-of-pearl buttons. One last time he double checked the room and examined the door before retiring to bed.

He was exhausted emotionally, physically and mentally, from the fatigues of the day, the dull conversations he had endured and now the lateness of the hour. And yet, as much as he was in need of rest, the more he tried to relax and go to sleep, the more he thought about his plans for welfare reform. Over and over his mind returned to the opportunities it presented and the law of diminishing returns that blighted his endeavours.

After what seemed like an hour or more, he became despondent and feared that he was destined to lie awake until sun rise. This lack of control made him angry. He was not used to being denied and petulantly decided to defy sleep if it should choose to call upon him. Alas, he was infinitely more likely to fall asleep than he was to enter into the kingdom of heaven and, sure enough, he had barely had time to enjoy his new-found freedom before his head sank unwittingly into his pillow and his mind into a semi-conscious torpor.

In fact, he believed himself to be wide awake, even though, with his rodent-like eyes, he found it impossible to distinguish transparent windows from opaque walls. There was a reason for this, however, he was not looking out into his bedroom, but into his wine-cellar. Here the shadows were impenetrable and he could not see the casks, vaulted ceiling, walls or thick iron gates that protected his precious collection.

In private, Smith was an aficionado of affectation. He insisted on his wine being sorted according to the courses and meals they were intended to accompany: luncheon, dinner, meat, fish etc. More generally, he had an affection for Charles Heidsieck "Monopole" Champagne, Domaine Leflaive and Domaine Coche-Dury for whites and Chateau Leoville, Chateau Lafite and Mouton Rotchilde for red.

Originating from at least the sixteenth century, the vault was connected to the house via a spiral staircase, but Smith had no recollection of using it that night. He was, however, conscious of the chilled atmosphere, a consequence of being almost 100 yards below ground and a perfect characteristic for aging and stocking wine.

The casks were stored in the north facing tunnel and bottles in the south and here and there benches had been cut into the wall for use when tastings took place. It was on one such seat that his gaze came to rest upon a sight that caused great astonishment and an infernal dread. Now, Smith prided himself on the fact that he was not someone who was easily frightened but, on this occasion, he had to admit to himself that his blood ran cold.

At first, he was aware of some kind of supernatural light that sparkled green, red, yellow, blue and violet and appeared now as small patches of light, now as streamers, arcs, rippling curtains and shooting rays. With each passing phase, the recess shone with an incredible glow for an instant and then at another went dark. All these fluctuations made its occupant emerge and recede from view, as different parts of its body glistened, dissolved and melted away.

After what Smith felt to be an age, the vision became as distinct and clear as it was ever likely to be, but with a slimy greenish bloom that caused a sense of disgust and loathing. He could not say that he felt it himself, but the creature seemed to be wrapped in an unnatural atmosphere that caused its many legs to move independently of one another, while its body sat perfectly still. The complete image being one of a gluttonous caterpillar.

Its head, however, was almost human. Collar length hair had been dyed dark chestnut to conceal the whitening of age, glued straight at the sides and anchored above the forehead by a pair of spectacles. The eyes were fixed, glazed, black voids sunk into an iridescent, wrinkle free skin. Atop a square jaw sat a mouth in characteristic sulking pout.

It did not appear to be angry, in spite of its sullen expression and for a moment Smith thought he had seen it somewhere before. "Miller," he murmured "is that you?"

"It is" came a languid reply interrupted by the conversation it was having with a bunch of fresh summer flowers.

"What do you want with me?"

"It has come to my attention that you have been considering some new-born resolutions."

"Yes, that is true" Smith agreed and recounted his plans for bereaved families.

"Is that all?" chastised Miller. "I fear that you have spent too much time in the silent shadows of your study and lost the desire for wholehearted revenge."

"Did we not work well together, when we devised the bedroom tax and when as Minister for Destitution you helped to make it harder for sick and disabled people to claim benefits?

"Remember how we introduced capability assessments, so that we could force sick and disabled people to do unpaid work and strip them of benefits if they refused. A move so successful that thousands of malingerers chose to die rather than admit that they were fit for work. And was it not on United Nations' International Day of Persons with Disabilities that we announced this brave new world, together with testimonies from claimants thanking us for changing their lives?

"Yes, yes, but we should not become focused on detail ahead of outcomes. That way you risk becoming dry and withered among your dusty tomes."

"Miller" he said, imploringly "pretty fat caterpillar, speak comfort to me."

"You, miserable man!" shouted the larvae angrily and reared itself upright as it spoke. "It is time your spirit walked beyond the house of commons, beyond the narrow limits of that money-grubbing place and journeyed abroad. Your mortal life is too short to be wasted on such narrow confines. No amount of regret can make amends for opportunities missed."

Smith looked somewhat ashamed, as the caterpillar continued: "You must aim to paint upon a broader canvas to blight those who work hard to earn a scant reward. If they are cheerful and happy with their lives of labour, they must be too well protected. They have been too delicately nurtured and tenderly brought up without recourse to the whip of privation. What right have they to inner contentment and peace? What right to enjoy Nature at the expense of entrepreneurs who would drill, frack and mine in order to turn an honest profit? What right to selfishly oppose the creation and sale of animals and crops implanted with alien genes?"

"Don't be a tease Miller, tell me what I should do."

"I can no more tell you that, than I can explain how it is that I appear as this creature. Look to your window for answers, I cannot say more. I cannot stay, or linger here."

And with that the Caterpillar yawned, shook itself and crawled into the solid wall.

VIII

Smith turned to leave, but in doing so he only came face to face with his own bedroom window. The curtains had been drawn by some unseen hand, for Smith had closed them before he went to bed. He was sure of that.

This new arrangement allowed moonbeams to flood in through the upper part of the casement, but at eye level very little could be seen. Then, just as he was about to try and rub the frost off the glass, a noise broke forth outside. At first it seemed to accord with the quiet moonlight, but as he listened he became sensible of deep, dull, hollow, melancholy noises.

Instead of being close by they sounded as if they were at a distance, so he opened the window, slowly, gravely, silently, hoping to hear them more distinctly. Looking out he could not see anything and could only be sure that it was very foggy and extremely cold. Now the incoherent sounds began to grow to such a pitch that it seemed as if a mournful, wailing dirge of self-accusatory lamentation had taken possession of the world.

He became desperate to locate the source and losing all inhibition stuck his head out of the window. The air was filled with phantoms from the continental regions, bedecked in national costume they were being blown violently back and forth by strong winds upon the bleak, dark night. Ministers and governments were linked together in their restless haste, scattering gloom and misery as they went. He recognised many of them as the architects of European Union, some he had known personally and many were now in their graves.

Over time, the source of their misery became clear to him, they had sought to interfere, for gain, in human matters, and feared they might lose their power to other kinds of men. Which brought him back to his conversation with Miller. "What had she meant when she said: 'For your own sake, may you choose the liberal life and not make the mistake of dismissing me as an unprofitable dream'?"

The more he tried to solve the riddle, the more dismayed Smith became. He even began to quake with indignation. The Minister for Wrack and Ruin should not be treated in this way and it was all he could do to stop himself from losing his temper. But this was the very emotion he needed to unlock his devilish creativity.

Although he didn't like too much change, it wasn't the conservative way, he had to admit that he was far from content. He wanted to see quicker, better, more far reaching results from his reforms, but he was being held back by European directives and court decisions.

"So, that is what Miller meant!" he screeched in a tone of delight. "If I am to fulfil my ambition, Britain must leave the European Union!

"I will resign my position and be the first to speak out, so that it can be clear to all."

And so, he sat down to write his resignation letter. His hand was not steady, but he persevered, getting up and walking across the room several times to clear his head. He was so convinced by his new cause that he would brook no resistance and rebuff any adversary with a malice befitting only a satrap of the Devil, such as himself.

Such were the eccentricities and peculiar hobbies of Smith, that neither drink nor Christmas could have made him any the more implacable in his quest for perdition.

In fact, it might be said that he spent this, the most festive and sacred time of year, drawing up destructive plans to make Brexit a reality for all.

IX

Over the coming days, a strategy began to take shape. It was time to push the destruct button and invent himself anew. His first step would be to leave his post, so that he would be free to extol the supposed benefits of Brexit. Not that he would admit the reason, of course. In what appeared to be a stunning volt-face, he decided to cry foul over reductions in his departmental budget and sacrifice his position in a principled opposition to benefit cuts for the disabled. He didn't care if the world thought he was mad, for in his hypocrisy he was wont to wear a mask of goodness, and was a past master of saying whatever he liked and then believing it. In response to accusations that he was making things up, he would retort: "You cannot absolutely prove those things are connected and I believe this to be true."

Days became weeks, weeks merged into months and months into years, as Smith took pleasure as his latest plot unfolded. The Brexit referendum was won, the buffoon who had succeeded him was gone and replaced by an equally incompetent gurning gargoyle. Even his old familiar, McVain, whose parvenu impertinence he detested, had departed the scene; or, so he thought.

Now approaching the autumn of his days, he was almost contented to have come so far and enjoyed reflecting on all that he had achieved. In fact, it could never be said that he ever squandered an opportunity to experience a sense of fulfilment, as if imbibing in a rich and sweet elixir, when recalling how: the unfair pension system was changed to make people work harder, for longer instead of enjoying retirement; the Universal Penury scheme forced people to work for their benefits or have them withdrawn for three years, and ensured that low earners must take more than one job to reduce their reliance on state handouts. His favourite motto being: 'We won't just give you hardworking taxpayers money, you'll have to work for it.'

He also introduced a benefits cap, that would see families homeless and children in poverty, if they did not work, but was indignant when the intended effects of food poverty and hunger were ameliorated by a scandalous rise in the number of foodbanks. Such philanthropy he saw as causing a new form of dependency that bred anti-social behaviour and low self-esteem, when what was needed was the discipline of destitution, hardship and hopelessness. He condemned such charity, as deeply unfair, as wasting a potential opportunity to balance the books on the backs of the poor and vulnerable, and as uniting society instead of sowing division.

But all that was about to change with Brexit, when the right people would take back control, and do away with nonsensical rights and regulations. Alas, there would be no chance for his departmental fellow travellers to hold parties to celebrate the success of incremental reductions in welfare provision. No more would there be a need to employ bailiffs to collect overpayments made in error by his old department. If all went well, no payments would be made at all.

Smith, however, was never one to live without perspective. He welcomed such developments as a reward for past endeavours and as an opportunity to become ever more introspective. In the even-tide of life, he expected to bask in the warm glow of appreciation that others would show for his deeper and higher wisdom. This would be his secret, a self-contained pleasure that would be shared with no one. It would be hidden behind a horny outer shell, in much the same way as the purpose of his earlier deeds had been concealed behind an avuncular appearance.

At least, that was the plan, but Smith was not the first to learn that even the most accomplished operator cannot control their future. In reality, he was no different to any other mortal, always standing at the edge of the unknown, unable to predict what would befall them. Perhaps that is why he was still troubled by a terrible foreboding that the reputation he had rescued from the ashes of his own failings and nurtured on revenge, was in danger of tumbling, Icarus-like, back into oblivion.

Could it be, that all he had achieved and accumulated, was now threatened by the hubris of a half-witted Cabinet? Believing themselves to be invincible, they had not only lost a general election, but had given McVain a way back into Parliament. And worse still, the infighting and ineptitude of this misanthropic menagerie had gifted his old fiefdom of Wrack and Ruin to this arriviste northerner.

Now, it should be acknowledged that Smith had not bestowed a single thought on McVain for many months, but of his antipathy toward her, there can be no doubt. After all, she had none of his finesse. Her eyes exhibited a resentment of everyone and everything and the curve of her mouth bore the unmistakeable wrinkle of the hypocrite. Some of a more generous disposition suggested that she had softened in her ways but, if that was so, it was only because the icicles within had dissolved into a lake of vile slush that is the product of sleeting rain. Indeed, on the surface, her demeanour was still that of a restless person, led only by desire for worldly pleasures. As she herself was fond of saying: 'People always want something for nothing.'

Smith could live with her propensity to mislead Parliament, after all that was the job of a

Government Minister. And he himself was a master of the dark arts. On the contrary, it was her lack of artifice that depressed him most. She seemed incapable of exhibiting indifference to those suffering extreme hardship. With all the subtlety of a ferocious polecat she revelled in it: "I am not oblivious to people who are incredibly vulnerable or who are in need. Indeed, I like to encourage constituents to describe their suffering to me in surgeries."

And "If a woman is to be granted tax credits after having more than two children, she will have to prove that conception was not consensual. It is only right and proper that they explain their ordeal in order to access benefits. After all, we can't deliver well deserved tax cuts for the richest without cutting support for the poorest ... It makes no sense to say that someone with nothing can be worse off."

It was the unbridled hostility exhibited in outbursts such as these that disturbed the very marrow in Smith's bones, made his skin crawl, literally. You see Smith had noticed something quite disturbing of late. He was becoming conscious of a kind of dread that, instead of savouring his achievements, he was simply clinging on to them, hoping that his legacy would not be undone by McVain's wrathful profligacy.

It happened gradually at first, that when catching his reflection in a mirror or window, he noticed a change in the pallor of his skin. Quite by chance, he thought he was beginning to resemble Matthias Grünewald's diseased Christ. Then at other times, the face was gaunt with grey wispy hair, not dissimilar to his constituency's previous representative and his mentor the esteemed Baron Chingford. The odd thing was, however, that no one else seemed to notice. At least, if they did, they did not mention it.

As his unease grew, so the caricature seemed to develop. He was filled with a terror that he, of all people, had a conscience after all and that others should become aware of it. It brought melancholy where formerly there had been power, passion and aliveness. The mere thought of it began to make him doubt his former view on life. He was even kept awake at night, sobbing violently until his face was wet with tears, by the monstrous notion that once again he would have to suffer public shame and, even worse, have to make public atonement.

In an attempt to banish his demons, he resolved not to leave his mansion, had all mirrors removed and shutters drawn across the windows. And yet, in spite of all these precautions, which it might be said made shaving an uneasy task, he could not resist the occasional temptation to observe his reflection in a secret room, in which he kept the only mirror in the whole house. It was just to make sure it wasn't all a figment of his imagination, you understand, but unfortunately for Smith, he was not a man of strong imagination.

Each time he yielded, he was doomed to look fixedly at the same phenomenon and succumb to the chilling influence of its glazed, death-like eyes. Incredulous, his blood curdled as he fought against his senses and examined the rear of the mirror in search of an imposter. And each time his half-expected disappointment was fulfilled, he let out a cry that was horrible in its agony.

It was as if some terrible disease had made his face as pale as death, withered, wrinkled and loathsome. He was tormented by the thought these reflections were windows on a monstrous soul-life, a hideous warning that he would never be at peace. That for what was left of his life, he would be persecuted by a nightmare of his own creation. As if his earthly body was little more than an un-consecrated corpse, whose appearance belied its true state of putrefaction.

Rather than suffer this fate, he thought he would rather hang from a tree and be fed upon by harpies, or be chased and torn to pieces by dogs. The more he thought about it, the more Smith trembled and sat in mournful meditation of his fate. To spend the rest of his days with no rest, no peace, only incessant torture, was not an agreeable idea. He fell upon his knees, clasping his hands to his face, as his mind turned to fog, a dingy cloud obscuring anything that might give succour. There was nothing that he could do that would cleanse him of this suffocating shroud.

For the first time in a long while, he felt unable to take comfort in anything. Even though he subscribed to the view that life should be more precious the less of it there is left live, he could not live up to this credo, because he could not be certain when his fire would go out. Without doubt, he would have poked it out, if he could be sure it would extinguish his last frail spark forever, but it seemed that larger forces were at work, shaping his destiny.

Gone were his anger, selfishness and coldness. He was barely able to muster a sullen, gurgling murmur of defiance. It had never been his way to give up or resign himself to misfortune, but he could do nothing now. All that was left was to look squarely ahead at the inevitability of this enduring malady, which no unhallowed hand could disturb. In the end, he was to be perpetually sensible of his own wretched, abject, frightful, hideous, miserable self, now and for always.

Amen.

Printed in Great Britain
by Amazon